D1395627

This Little Tiger book belongs to:

_____

_____

_____

_____

_____

To Bridie
A.M.

To Alice, with love
G.W.

LITTLE TIGER PRESS
An imprint of Magi Publications
1 The Coda Centre, 189 Munster Road
London SW6 6AW
www.littletigerpress.com
First published in Great Britain 1998
This edition published 2004
Text copyright © Alan MacDonald 1998
Illustrations copyright © Gwyneth Williamson 1998
Alan MacDonald and Gwyneth Williamson have asserted their rights to be identified as the author and illustrator of this work under the Copyright, Designs and Patents Act, 1988
A CIP catalogue record for this book is available from the British Library
All rights reserved
ISBN 1 84506 068 7
Printed in China
2 3 4 5 6 7 8 9 10

BEWARE of the BEARS!

by Alan MacDonald

illustrated by Gwyneth Williamson

LITTLE TIGER PRESS
London

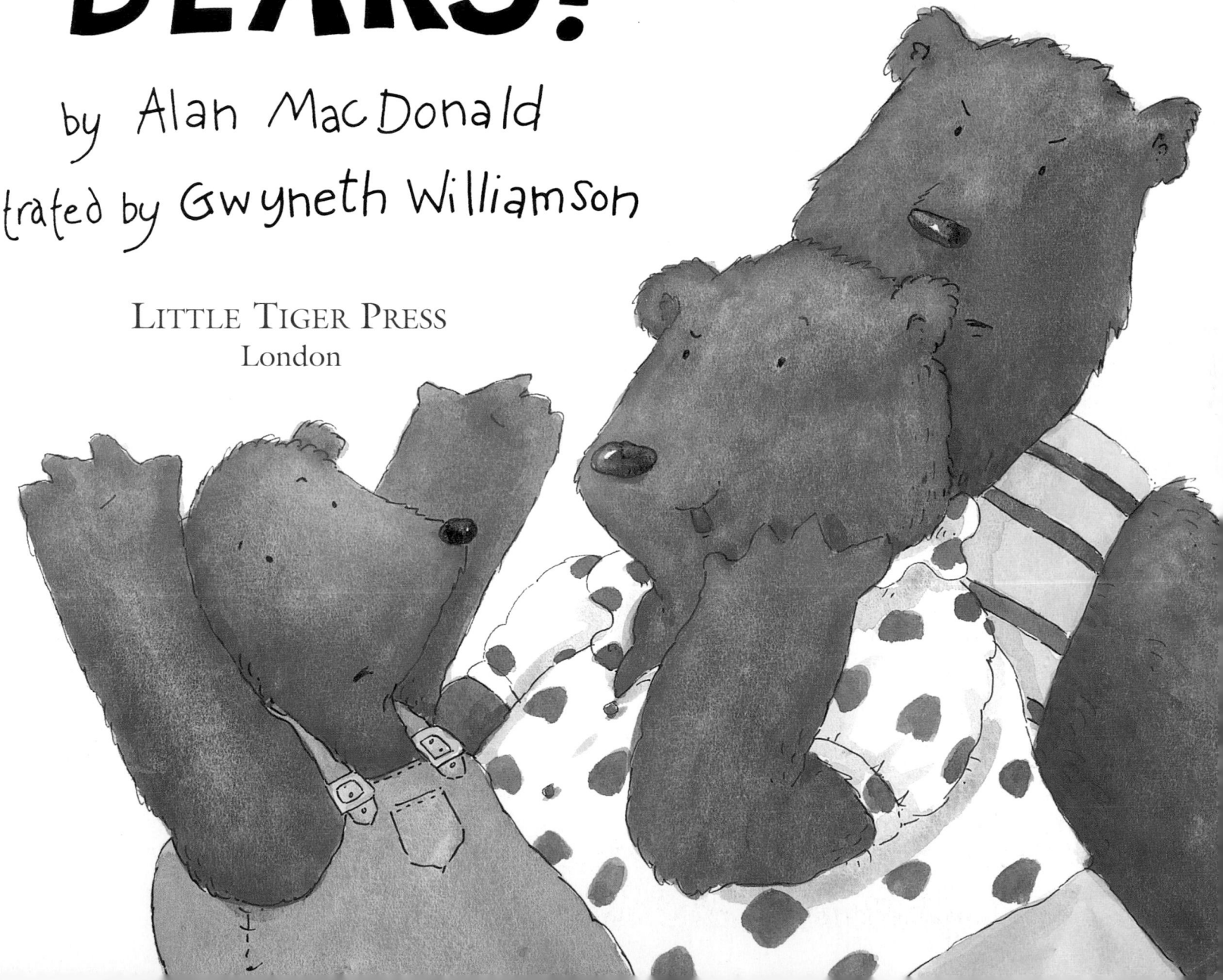

When the three bears saw what Goldilocks had done to their little cottage, they were hopping mad.
Their porridge eaten!
Chairs broken!
Beds bounced on!
"Go after her! Find out where she lives!" ordered Daddy Bear.

Baby Bear jumped on his scooter and sped after Goldilocks.

In no time at all he was back.
"She lives on the far side of the forest,"
panted Baby Bear. "And what's more,
she's just gone out again and left
her door unlocked."
"Good!" said Mummy Bear.
"What are we waiting for?
Let's see how *she* likes having
uninvited guests."

Baby Bear led the way through the forest to Goldilocks' cottage. The door was unlocked, just as he'd said.

On the breakfast table were several open packets.
"This isn't porridge," sniffed Mummy Bear.
Baby Bear read the labels. "Wheetos, Munch Flakes and Puffo Pops."
"Sounds all right to me," said Daddy Bear. "Pour away, Baby-o!"

"These Wheetos are too sweet," said Daddy Bear.
"These Munch Flakes are too noisy," said Mummy Bear.
"But these Puffo Pops are just right," said Baby Bear, catapulting a spoonful towards Daddy Bear.

A Puffo Pop hit Daddy Bear in the eye. He sent back a spoonful of Wheetos. They splattered all over Mummy Bear's best blouse.
Soon cereal was flying left and right, till the carpet, the walls and the ceiling were dripping with brown goo.

Baby Bear turned on the radio.
"Let's dance!" he squealed.

Mummy and Daddy Bear tangoed on the table.
"This table's too slippy," said Daddy Bear.

They did the cha-cha round the curtains. "These curtains are too rippy," said Mummy Bear.

"But this sofa's just right," squeaked Baby Bear, so they all jumped on the sofa and did the bossa nova until . . .

. . . they went right through it!

Next the three bears looked upstairs.
There were lots of things to try
in the bathroom.
"The shaving soap's too soapy,"
grumbled Daddy Bear.

"This toothpaste's
too minty," gargled
Mummy Bear.

"But this bubble bath is
just right," murmured Baby
Bear from beneath a
mountain of suds.
"All right, here we come,"
said Mummy Bear . . .

SPLASH!

They had a splashing
time in the bath
and . . .

. . . once they were clean and the bathroom a mess,
off they went to the bedroom.
"These pyjamas are too tight," said Daddy Bear,
bursting the buttons.
"This mattress is too
lumpy," said Mummy
Bear, bouncing up
and down.
"But these pillows are
just right," said Baby
Bear. "Just right for
a pillow fight."

Baby Bear biffed Mummy Bear. Mummy Bear whacked Daddy Bear. Pillows burst, filling the air with clouds of feathers. Till suddenly Daddy Bear stopped. "Listen!" he said. "I hear someone." Quietly, the three bears crept downstairs . . .

Goldilocks was in the kitchen.
Gleefully, Daddy Bear, Mummy Bear and Baby Bear watched from behind the door.
Goldilocks gasped when she saw the cereal splattered all over the walls.

Her eyes grew large when she saw the ripped curtains and the gigantic hole in the sofa.

She whistled when she saw the bathroom flooded with water and decorated with shaving foam.

Next Goldilocks went into the bedroom. She stared open-mouthed at the sea of feathers and the burst bedsprings. Then suddenly the three bears jumped out from behind the door.

"Surprise!" they all shouted.
"We thought *we'd* pay *you* a visit,"
added Mummy Bear.
Goldilocks looked at them,
then at the room . . .

. . . and to the bears' astonishment, she threw back her head and laughed and laughed until her hair shook like golden springs.
"But aren't you mad at what we've done to your house?" asked Daddy Bear.
"*My* house? This isn't my house," giggled Goldilocks.
"But it must be," said Baby Bear, "I saw you go in."
"Oh that," said Goldilocks. "The door was open, so I thought I'd have a nose around. I'm always sneaking into other people's houses. I only came back because I left Teddy behind."

"Then – if it's not your house, *whose house is it?*" asked Daddy Bear. "Oh help!" squeaked Baby Bear, looking out of the window . . .

BEWARE of the BIG BAD WOLF!

Books to make you giggle, from Little Tiger Press

For information regarding the above titles or for our catalogue, please contact us: Little Tiger Press,
1 The Coda Centre, 189 Munster Road, London SW6 6AW
Telephone: 020 7385 6333 Fax: 020 7385 7333
Email: info@littletiger.co.uk www.littletigerpress.com